The *Extraordinary*

retold by Letta Schatz   illustrated by John Burningham

FOLLETT PUBLISHING COMPANY   *Chicago   New Yor*

Tug-of-War

T/L 2339

This Book is dedicated to

the countless talented tellers of tales who made this story

and changed this story as they passed it ever on—

from mouth to ear, from old to young,

from village to village, in many tongues

across the width of their great continent—Africa.

Long ago, before your father's father's father's father was born, Hare, Hippopotamus, and Elephant were neighbors in the great green woods by the wide brown river.

7

Hippopotamus and Elephant were forever teasing poor Hare, because they were bigger. They were unbearably boastful and rude.

"Oh, Hare," Hippopotamus would hoot from his snoozing place in the river's cool ooze. "You are so little, if you fell into the river, you would not make a splash. Not even a ripple."

8

And Elephant would bellow, billowing with laughter,
"Ho, Hare! I hear you are called 'Big Ears!' Big Ears! You!
Please look at ME! One ear of mine would make a tent for
ten like you!"

"And how comically you move," Hippopotamus would
snort. "Hoppity-hop! Poor Hare! Your feet can barely stay on
the ground. You are so light a sneeze could easily blow you
away!"

"True! True! Hoppity-Hare hardly leaves a track. The
grass does not even bend when he passes!" Elephant would
trumpet his agreement. "When WE pass, trees tremble and
crash. OUR feet leave holes so deep, Hare could fall in and
never be seen."

And so it went. Day after day Hare bore the teasing.
But at last, the day came when he had borne all that he could.
Hare determined to get even. He would show Hippopotamus
and Elephant that size was not all that mattered.

Hare thought and thought. His ears wiggled. His nose
twitched. And at last, the great idea was hatched.

Hare went to see Hippopotamus in his snoozing place in
the cool brown river.

"Greetings to you, Hippopotamus," Hare began politely.

"Oh, small, insignificant speck," Hippopotamus heaved. "How dare you address your bigger and better?"

"If I can win over you in a tug-of-war, will you admit that I am your equal?" asked Hare.

"YOU? Win over ME? In a tug-of-war? RIDICULOUS!" snorted Hippopotamus. "I am twenty-million-trillion times stronger. Look at me! How huge beside a puny runt like you!"

"Perhaps I have strengths that you cannot see," said Hare, and he hid a smile. "Will you agree to the tug-of-war?"

"If you wish," Hippopotamus shrugged. "I have nothing special to do today."

"Fine," said Hare. "I have here a very long, very strong rope. You will hold one end, and I will hold the other. I will go to my home in the woods. Then I will pull, and you will pull. If you can pull me into the river, then you, of course, will be the winner. But if I can pull you into the woods, then I will be the winner. And you must agree to call me your equal. Do you agree?"

"I agree," Hippopotamus said, in his most superior voice.

"Then hold the rope firmly in your mouth. When I reach my home in the woods, I will give a tug to show that I am ready to begin," said Hare.

Holding his end of the rope, Hare made his way deep, deep into the woods, to the place where Elephant made his home.

15

"Greetings to you, Elephant," Hare began politely.

Elephant elevated his trunk most haughtily. "Oh, tiny mite, almost hidden from sight, whom do you address? Mighty ME?" he asked.

"If I can win over you in a tug-of-war, will you admit that I am your equal?" asked Hare.

"Ho, Hare! Humorous Hare! That's the funniest joke I've heard in a year!" Elephant billowed and swelled with laughter. "YOU? Win over ME? In a tug-of-war? I am six thousand times bigger and a billion times stronger!"

"Perhaps I have strengths that you cannot see," said Hare. And this time he could not hide his smile. "Will you agree to the tug-of-war?"

Elephant shrugged eloquently. "I agree. Easiest contest I ever entered."

"Fine," said Hare. "I have here a very long, very strong rope. I will go down to the river. Then I will give a tug on the rope to show that I am ready. If you can pull me to your place in the woods, you will be winner. But if I can pull you into the river, then I will be winner. And you must agree to call me your equal."

Looking quite bored, Elephant took hold of his end of the rope.

Hare started back toward the river, laughing so heartily he could hardly hop. When he was halfway between Elephant and Hippopotamus, Hare stopped.

Hare gave a great tug on the rope.
The extraordinary tug-of-war began.

19

Hippopotamus in the river's ooze felt Hare's tug and
began to pull.

Elephant at his home in the woods felt Hare's tug and began to pull.

Each thought he was pulling against little Hare. Each expected to win easily. A tug or two and Hare would come flying, like a tiny fish on a fisherman's line.

Hippopotamus tugged and Elephant tugged. The rope grew tighter. But nothing happened. Neither budged.

Hippopotamus pulled harder.

Elephant pulled harder.

Each thought, surely now Hare will come flying to me. Ridiculous Hare with his foolish dare. How could he possibly be the equal of powerful me!

They pulled and pulled. They pulled all day while the sun rode high.

They pulled at sunset.

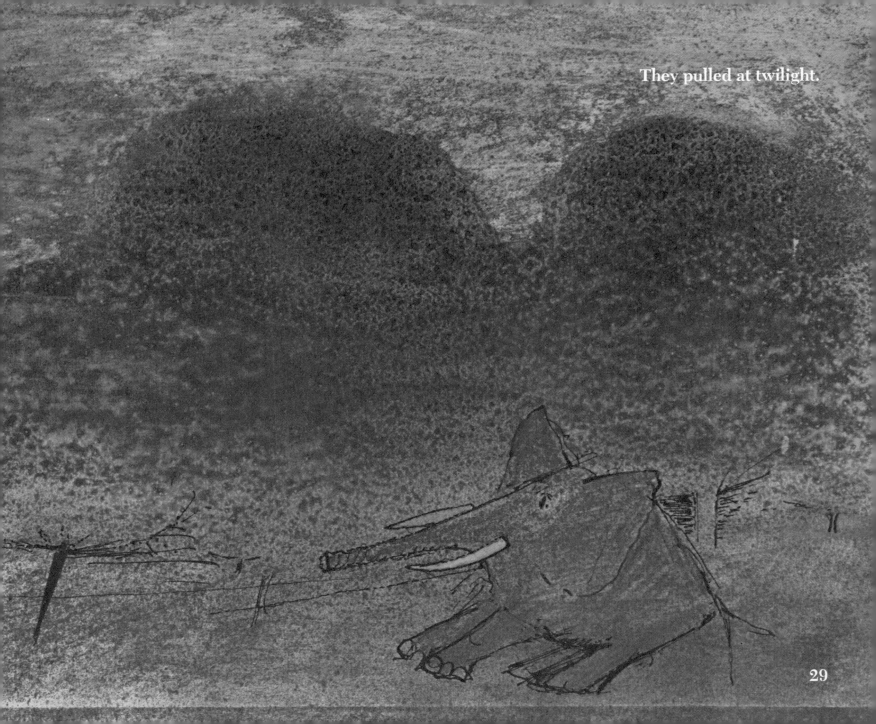

They pulled at twilight.

29

They pulled and pulled through the long moonlit night.
But the rope remained taut as before. Each could not believe
that he could not budge little Hare.

Hippopotamus dug his feet deep into the river bottom and tugged and tugged and tugged. He churned up great brown billows of mud. The wide brown river grew browner than ever. But still the rope stayed taut. Hippopotamus pondered.

Elephant swelled his chest. He pulled on his
end with all his strength. His feet made great
grooves in the forest floor.
Why didn't Hare budge? Elephant wondered.

33

And all day, through sunset and twilight and night, as
Hippopotamus and Elephant pulled and puzzled, Hare rested.
He watched the taut rope and laughed. And laughed. And
laughed and laughed.

35

At last, just before dawn, Hare crept close to the river's edge and hid in the brush. Making his voice sound soft and drawn out and far away, he called, "O-o-o-h, Hippo-pot-a-mus, would you like to stop? I am still strong and fit. But if you wish to stop, I will. You need only admit that I am your equal."

"Im-pos-sible!" puffed Hippopotamus. "Pre—pos—ter— ous! Never will I admit it! Puny you the equal of me? Never!"

And Hippopotamus heaved on the rope even harder than before.

36

Smiling to himself, Hare hopped silently back through the woods, till he neared Elephant's clearing. He hid behind a great mahogany tree and called in his soft, faraway voice, "O-o-h, El-e-phant! Would you like to stop? I am still strong and fit. But if you wish to stop, I will. You need only admit that I am your equal."

"NEV—ER!" Elephant bellowed. "Tiny, insignificant you the equal of mighty me! Never, never, NEV—ER!"

37

And Elephant swelled and reared back in rage and pulled
a great full-strength elephant pull. AND Hippopotamus was
pulled right out of the river. Huge and ponderous
Hippopotamus ploughed a deep furrow in the sandy bank.
He crushed the brush along the shore. His huge belly was
scraped and sore.

Hippopotamus grew enormously angry. He puffed and pawed and snorted and roared. He leaned back and heaved on the rope, eleven times harder than before.

Hippopotamus' huge heave pulled Elephant smashing past the edge of his clearing. Elephant was hauled through thickets and tangled in creepers and smashed into trees that crashed upon him.

How Elephant raged! How he strained and wrenched on the rope!

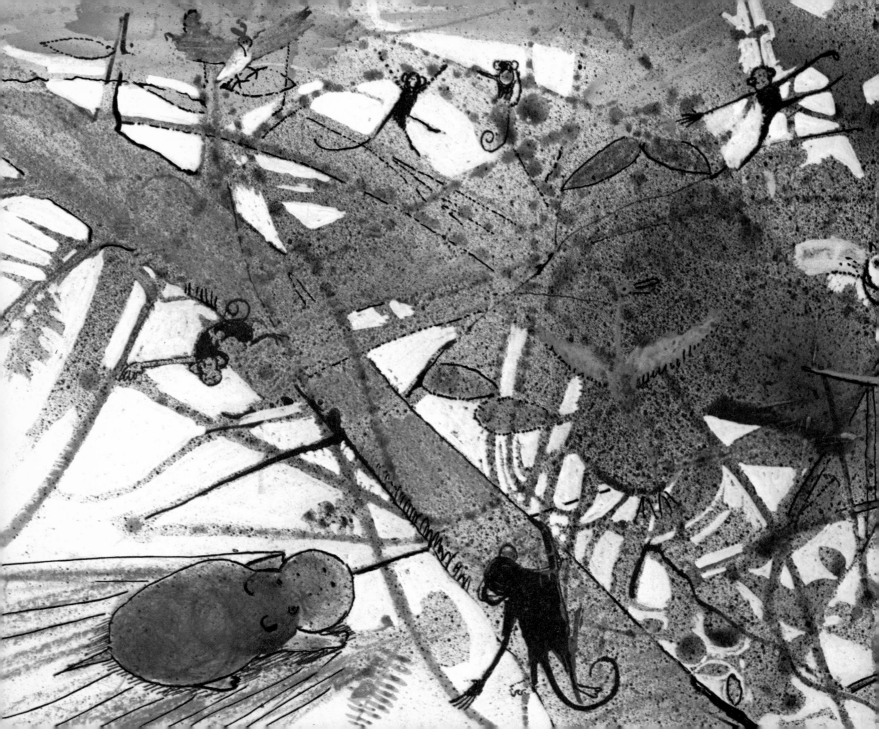

Now the battle grew truly furious. The two great beasts bellowed and stormed. Backwards and forwards they dragged each other. They battled all day while the sun rode high. They battled at sunset. They battled at twilight. They battled and battled through the long, moonlit night.

Time after time, Hippopotamus was hauled roaring from the water. The riverbed was churned into a thick brown sludge of mud. The river was scalloped with canals dug by his body.

Time after time, Elephant was dragged crashing through the woods. Such a shambles! Everywhere there were trampled thickets, scattered branches, toppled trees.

43

As the great beasts battled, Hare relaxed. He watched the rope. And laughed and chuckled and giggled and rolled and guffawed.

Again, before dawn, Hare crept close to each of the two great beasts and called to each in turn, "Would you like to stop? Do you not agree that I am your equal?"

Hippopotamus huffed and wheezed as he wearily heaved on the rope. He slipped in the sludge and floundered about.

Elephant sagged, bruised and battered. He could barely manage to stand.

But both were too stubborn to stop. Neither would admit that Hare was his equal. They wearily pulled as the sun rose higher. They wearily pulled and wearily wondered. How could Hare manage to pull so long? Could he possibly be so strong?

Surely Hare is using magic. I must see for myself. Hippopotamus grunted. He heaved himself out of the river and cautiously started toward the place where he would find Hare. Every few feet he stopped to take a loop in the rope so that it would stay as taut as before.

44

Elephant, too, was deeply baffled. He decided to see for himself. Stopping every few feet to draw the rope tight, Elephant slowly lumbered through the woods, toward the place where he would find Hare.

The two great beasts came toward each other, closer and closer, with the rope tight between them. In the middle of the woods, Elephant and Hippopotamus met. They stood. They stared. They glared at each other.

"Meddling Elephant!" roared Hippopotamus. "What are you doing with that rope? How dare you interfere?"

"Interfere!" bellowed Elephant. "What of yourself? I was having a tug-of-war with Hare! Explain what you are doing here!"

They stared. They glared. And then suddenly they knew. The two great beasts realized that they had been tricked. Tricked by little Hare.

They stormed through the woods, hunting for Hare. They stamped and trampled and smashed and thrashed and thundered and blundered and raged and roared. But not one hair of Hare did they find.

Hare, already far, far away, was hopping along in search
of a new home. He was smiling to himself because, small
as he was, he had outwitted Hippopotamus and Elephant,
the biggest beasts of all.

48